PIRATES, PREDATORS AND PENGUINS

Further Adventures With Zak and Rory

Written by
Geoff Swift

Illustrated by Jane Cornwell

JC STUDIO Press

Published in 2021 by JC STUDIO Press
Design and Illustration by Jane Cornwell
www.janecornwell.co.uk

ISBN: 978-1-7399088-2-9

Dedication

To Grant and Beth, who a few years ago ask their mum if I could write a story about pirates. So, when I had 'writer's block' your request came to mind. I hope you enjoy the story.

Geoff Swift

To Geoff and Rona Swift, thank you very much for all of your support and encouragement.

Jane Cornwell

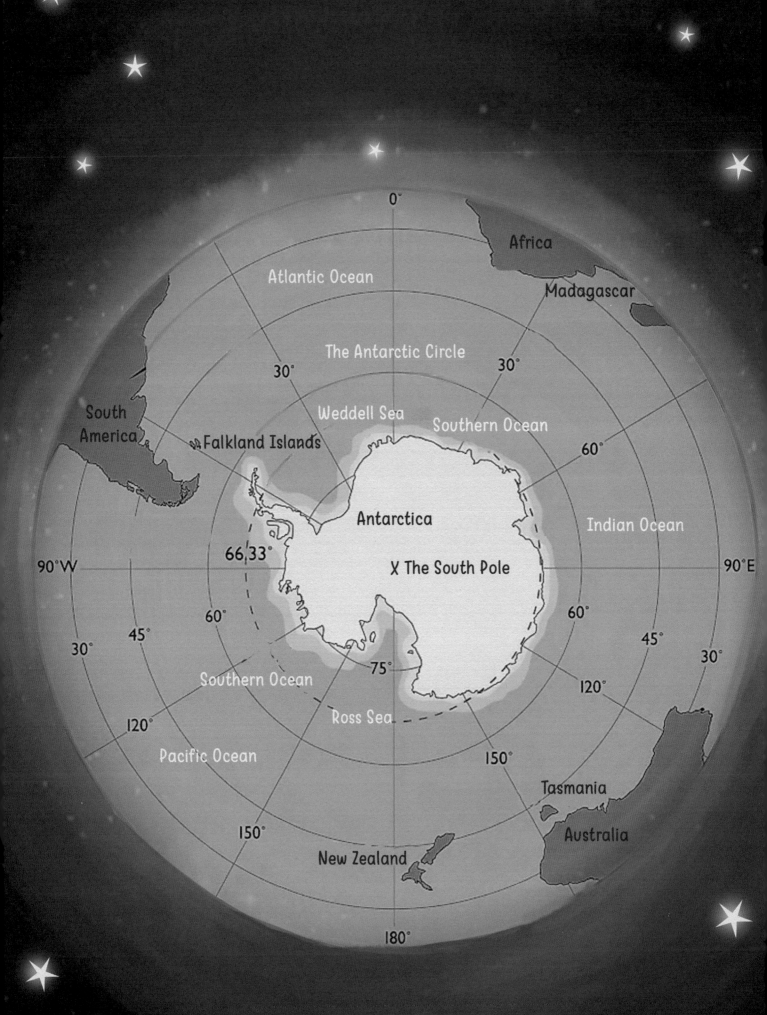

Contents

Chapter 1

Zak and I had been drifting and swimming off the South Island of New Zealand, which the humans call The Land of the Long White Cloud, for three months, ever since Zak had been attacked, harpooned, and injured by Japanese whalers. After I had rescued Zak, I disabled the whaler's ship by jamming the harpoon they had attacked Zak with in the ship's propeller. We had slowly made our way here, so Zak could rest and recover from his injuries. We swam in the Foveaux Strait between New Zealand's Fiordland and Stewart Island. Zak had chosen to come here as he knew the waters were quiet and he could rest but it also offered us a quick escape route to either the Tasman Sea or The South Pacific Ocean. We rested in Te Waewae, Colac, and Toetoes Bays where there were very few humans and Zak felt safe.

I should also explain who we are, my friend Zak is a Sperm Whale, and I am called Rory and I am a Plesiosaur. Zak and I had met off the west coast of Scotland and had become good friends and agreed to travel the world's oceans together. During our travels, I had met Zak's family and some of his friends. Zak and I had also shared a few adventures and close encounters with humans, so we were enjoying a relaxing time.

One day we were floating on the surface of the water enjoying the warm summer sun when we heard a shout.

'Zak! Rory!'

Zak and I looked at each other with puzzled looks, no one knew we were here. Once again there was a shout.

'Zak! Rory!'

I raised my head on my long neck while Zak flipped eight metres out of the water, both of us looking around for the voice but there was nothing to be seen.

Zak looked at me and spoke. 'It must have been the wind. There's no-one and nothing to be seen for miles.' He just finished speaking when once again we heard a shout.

'Zak! Rory! Up here you idiots.' Zak and I both looked up, there flying over us was Owen the Albatross. He floated lower towards us, his massive three-metre wings spread out and wingtips feathered as he glided down. He slowly circled so we could follow him without becoming dizzy.

'I'm glad I found you, I've got a message from Lewis, he needs your help.'

I looked at Owen then turned Zak and asked, 'Who is Lewis?'

Zak looked up at Owen and nodded that he understood the message, then faced me. 'Lewis is an Emperor Penguin who lives in the Antarctic. If he's asking for my help, then his colony of penguins must be in trouble.'

Zak looked from me to Owen, 'Owen, did he say what was wrong?'

Owen slowed his circular glide, then came in lower, skimming the surface almost touching the water then answered Zak. 'Spike and his gang of Orca killer whales. They've been attacking and terrorising the Emperors. Every time they go to the ice edge to enter the water with their chicks, Spike and his gang attack. There are thousands of Emperors mustered along the ice edge, but they are frightened to go into the water. Can you help him Zak?'

Zak looked at me smiled, then looked up at Owen. 'I think we can sort Spike out ok. Rory has had a few run-ins with Spike and Spike owes Rory a few favours, in fact, they are almost friends. Owen, could you do us a favour? Could you fly ahead and let Lewis know we're leaving now, and we'll be there in two days.'

Once again Owen skimmed in low over us then shouted. 'I'm on my way. I'm also going to hang around when I get there to see what you do. This should be fun. It beats flying and gliding around the Southern Oceans day after day looking for action. See you in two days.'

With that Owen beat his giant wings and climbed up into the clear blue sky.

I looked at Zak and asked. 'Are you recovered enough to swim for two days?'

Zak shook his giant head and let out a chuckle that vibrated the water around him. 'Rory, I could swim for two weeks and hundreds of miles nonstop to see the surprise on Spike's face when we turn up. Come on let's go, we could do with some fun, we've rested long enough in New Zealand.'

With that, Zak turned, beat his giant fluke and he started swimming off towards the Antarctic ice fields with me alongside.

I didn't know at the time, but we were heading to a continent larger than Europe and almost double the size of Australia. I had been to the Arctic with Zak, but I was still amazed as we neared the ice, the brightness reflecting from the ice and the size of the landscape amazed me. I stopped swimming to raise my long neck to look around, I was in awe of the majesty of the surroundings. I was looking at the continent that contained ninety percent of the Earth's ice.

I slowly lowered my neck and looked at Zak and spoke. 'This place is amazing. I've seen snow and ice at home in Scotland and in the Arctic, but this is so much bigger, brighter and I think whiter, with hints of blue. Amazing.'

Zak smiled at me replying, 'Everything is different here compared to the Artic. Wait till you meet the penguins.'

I looked at Zak and asked him to tell me about Lewis and the Emperor penguins.

Zak slowed down and turned to face me. 'The Emperors are the tallest of the penguins, but they are only about one point two metres tall. They are also very tough and resilient to live in the Antarctic where the temperature can drop to sixty degrees centigrade below freezing, you just can't imagine how cold that is. But they live through these conditions. I think they also look quite cute. They are black with a white stomach and yellow and gold markings on the sides of their heads and necks. One thing I love doing is swimming with them, they are fantastic in the water and amazingly fast swimmers. They can dive to five hundred metres and stay under the water for up to twenty minutes. They are really good fun to watch and swim with. Come on let's go and sort out Spike, then we can have some fun.'

With that, Zak turned and we swam off towards the ice shelf.

Chapter 2

Four hours later we saw the ice shelf. As we drew nearer, we could see what looked like a black and white wave with yellow flashes rippling along the edge. It was the Emperors, they were at the edge of the ice shelf trying to enter the water, but Spike and his gang of killer Orcas were patrolling along the water's edge forcing the Emperors back on to the ice. If it wasn't so serious that the Emperors were unable to fish in the water, the sight would have been magnificent.

As far as we could see along the ice edge were the Emperors. As they retreated up the ice from Spike and his gang, they created an illusion of a giant Mexican wave of black, white and yellow, rippling against the Antarctic white backdrop, it was amazing and quite mesmerising. I was in a trance looking at the sight when Zak spoke.

'Right Rory, let's sort this out, here's the plan.'

As Zak outlined his plan my grin got bigger. I only had one question. 'Are you sure it will work? No one will get hurt especially not the Emperors?'

Zak laughed. 'Rory, I've seen you do the move before, everything will be ok, come on let's go and have some fun at Spike's expense.'

High above, Owen had been circling looking out for Zak and I. When he saw us on the horizon, he drifted down to Lewis to tell him we were in the area. He then climbed high above to see what Zak and I were going to do. Below Spike and his gang were powering, leaping and twisting out of the water along the ice edge looking for Emperors in the water and forcing the Emperors back onto the ice.

Zak and I slowed our approach so not to alert Spike of our presence. When we were two kilometres away from Spike's gang we slowly submerged and slid under the turquoise blue waters out of sight.

Owen flew along the ice edge looking from side to side for any sight of Zak and I, he tried to work out where we would appear. Then it dawned on him, focus on Spike, surely whatever our plan was, it would centre around him. He spotted Spike among his gang, then slowly circled him. He had circled him several times when there was an explosion of water, then Spike appeared to fly out of the water.

Owen veered off as Spike headed towards him like a speeding missile. As he moved away, he glimpsed back towards Spike, then, did a double-take. I had Spike in a tight grip with my flippers and was flying out of the water. I grinned at Spike, the surprised look on his face was priceless. At our peak we were thirty metres above the water, then we headed down. As we descended I twisted and rotated Spike to change the angle of our descent, we were landing on the ice near the Emperors. Below the Emperors were waddling as fast as they could away from our landing spot.

Before I landed, I twisted again so Spike hit the ice with a loud thump with me on top of him. When the Emperors heard the thump, they turned back to look at the stranded Spike and I. Spike had taken a hard fall, which, with me landing on top of him had knocked the breath out of him. He lay on the ice dazed and out of breath.

I rolled off him onto the ice and gave him a glance, then looked closely at the Emperors.

One Emperor waddled out of the pack towards me, smiled and he spoke. 'Hi, you must be Rory, Zak's friend. I'm Lewis. Owen said Zak was coming with his friend Rory, but I didn't expect you to make such an entrance. How you soared out of the water with Spike was awesome. You must be immensely strong. We can't thank you and Zak enough. We've been pinned on the ice for weeks by Spike and his gang, they just won't let us get into the water, we were becoming desperate as we need to get into the water to feed. Anyway, where's Zak?'

Chapter 3

Spike's gang gathered in a circle with their heads out of the water looking at the stranded Spike.

They were so engrossed by what was happening to Spike when the water in the middle of the circle exploded and a giant rose into the air towering over them. Zak had arrived!

When Zak reached his maximum height, he looked around and saw me, Spike, and Lewis on the ice. He blew the water out of his blowhole, then fell back into the water creating a massive wave, spinning Spike's gang in a vortex of foaming water, Zak slowly swam to the ice edge where Lewis and I were waiting to meet him.

Zak was first to speak 'Hi Lewis, I see you've met Rory; did we get here in time?'

Lewis laughed, 'Zak what I've just witnessed by Rory and you was worth waiting for, there's not a lot happens in the Antarctic. What you and Rory have done will be talked about for years amongst the Emperors and go down in Emperor folklore.'

We were chatting and laughing when we were disturbed.

'OH! AH! OH! AH! STOP IT! GET OFF! OH! AH! STOP IT, THAT HURTS! LEAVE ME ALONE! OH! STOP IT, AH! RORY, ZAK! ANYONE? HELP!'

We stopped talking and looked at the noise. Spike was surrounded by the Emperors who were pecking him at with their sharp-pointed beaks. Spike's body was surrounded by a thick layer of blubber which insulated him from the cold and kept him warm, however, it must have felt as though he was being pricked by hundreds of pins. We burst out laughing at Spike's predicament.

'Lewis they're your friends, they're giving Spike some of his own medicine while he's defenceless, what do you want to do next?' Zak asked.

Lewis looked down to the ice while he contemplated what to do. After a few minutes, he looked at Zak and I and said. 'All we want is to get in the sea and swim without being chased. I'll go and speak to Spike.'

As Lewis started to waddle towards Spike, I started to follow when Zak spoke to me in a low voice.

'Rory, stay here, let him do it himself.'

I stopped, looked at Lewis, smiled, waddled across the ice, then slid into the water beside Zak. We both watched as Lewis approached Spike. As he waddled towards Spike, he told the Emperors to stop pecking and to stand back. When he reached Spike, he stood in front of him and started talking to him very quietly, so no one could hear. Spike was nodding his head in agreement. After several minutes Lewis called the Emperors to Spike. As we watched the Emperors lined up on Spike's side which was away from the water, turned around, then leaned their backs against him. At Lewis's command, they all pushed against Spike. They were pushing him across the ice back to the sea.

After half an hour and many rests, they had Spike at the ice edge where one last push would get him in the water. The Emperors stopped while Lewis spoke to Spike, Spike's head was nodding up and down in agreement at what was being said, Lewis gave Spike a friendly pat on the nose with his stubby wing, then shouted 'PUSH!' at the Emperors.

They gave Spike a final push and he fell into the water with a splash creating a big wave. Spike's gang had been watching and rushed over surrounding him.

Chapter 4

On cue as if a dam had burst, the giant Mexican wave of white, yellow and black rippled along the ice edge once more as the Emperors dived into the water.

Zak, Owen, and I watched as the Emperors hit the water like missiles, swimming like torpedoes, the water was a foaming mass of Emperors.

Zak and I swam slowly through the melee of Emperors and Spike's gang to reach Spike.

Zak spoke first. 'Well, Spike here we are again! When will you stop annoying other creatures, and making a nuisance of yourself?'

Spike hung his head then spoke. 'Guys, I'm sorry. I thought we were just having fun keeping the Emperors out of the water. I didn't realise how important it was for the Emperors to get into the water to feed, having been on the ice for so long. I didn't know that they spent the long winter months on the ice with no food looking after their chicks. I'm really sorry. I'll gather up my gang and leave.'

With that Spike turned gathered his gang slipped under the water and swam off.

Zak and I looked at each other, then I asked. 'Do you think Spike can keep out of trouble?'

Zak smiled, shook his head and replied. 'Not a chance, the next time we see him he'll be in trouble or creating it. It's in his character, however, most of the time he's just a nuisance.'

As Zak was speaking Lewis had swum over to join us.

Zak smiled at Lewis then asked, 'Lewis, do you want to tell me what you said to Spike?'

Lewis looked serious as he thought about Zak's question. 'I asked him how it felt to be pecked by the penguins. He told me it was very sore, and he didn't want to be pecked again. I then told him, because of Rory isolating him on the ice and us causing him pain by our pecking we could isolate him from his gang and do the same in the water. So, if he or his gang came back to terrorise us, all the Emperors would dive into the water and attack him and his gang and peck them. He didn't like the idea, so he promised to leave and not come back.

Chapter 5

Zak and I watched as the Emperors enjoyed the freedom of getting in and out of the water whenever they wanted. It was amazing to watch. They looked as if they were flying when they flew out of the water onto the ice, then they would waddle around the ice. It was when they were in the water that they took my breath away. I thought Zak and I were good swimmers but the Emperors in the water were amazing.

As they swam around us, they would fly out of the water onto Zak's back using him as a big island to rest on. They would waddle along his back then dive into the water; everyone was having great fun. Sometimes they would have a competition to see who could fly out of the water right over Zak's big back and dive into the water on his other side.

As I watched it reminded me of the fun we had with one of our friends, Rodger (Rog) the Leatherback Turtle who travelled with us for a while. At one point, Zak and I came up with an idea to make Rog fly. As I watched Zak and the Emperor's I had an idea.

I was mulling over the idea when I was aware that Lewis was looking at me. I gave him a smile then he asked, 'Rory, I've been watching you and it looks as if you're planning something, what's going on?'

I let out a chuckle and said, 'How would you like to fly?'

Lewis lay back in the water and looked at me, 'Are you serious? Penguins have wings, but they are so short, we can't fly. Our short wings make us very manoeuvrable in the water but they are too little for us to fly'.

I laughed and said, 'If you are adventurous and trust Zak, we have a trick that can make you fly, it will be a short flight, but you'll fly. Are you game to try?'

Lewis burst out laughing, 'Rory, flying even for a short time would be fantastic, what do I need to do?' I called Zak over and whispered to him while Lewis and the rest of the Emperors, who heard Lewis and I talking, looked on. Zak gave one of his huge grins and said, 'Come on let's do it, this is going to be great fun. I'll position myself while you get the Emperors organised.'

With that Zak positioned himself, lying on the surface, facing away from the ice edge. I organised the Emperors into groups of ten and positioned them with their bodies vertically in the water behind Zak and over his fluke.

'Right Zak,' I shouted. There was a prolonged pause, the Emperors started looking around in anticipation. Suddenly there was a loud roar! The water around the Emperors exploded ten metres into the air. The Emperors flew out of the water, thrown in the air by Zak's fluke!

As they flew upwards, they were flapping their tiny wings trying to fly higher. After eighty metres they reached the zenith of their flight then they started gliding back towards the water. They entered the water with barely a ripple.

Suddenly there was pandemonium in the water, the Emperors who had flown were so excited they couldn't stop talking, meanwhile, the rest of the Emperors were desperately queuing up to have their turn at flying.

After five hours and thousands of flying Emperors, Zak was exhausted. We gathered along the ice edge with Zak resting in the water and the Emperors gathered on the ice edge. Each of the Emperors was discussing their flight, how it felt to be flying high above the water, arguing about who had flown the highest and longest.

The next day we repeated the process so by the end of the second day thousands of Emperors had 'flown'. At the end of the day when things had quietened, and everyone was resting, Zak glided over to me.

'Rory, I think we should leave tomorrow and continue our travels, the exercise I've had the last two days has shown me I'm fit to travel. Are you OK with that?'

I looked at Zak and at the Emperors before I spoke. 'I'll miss my new friends and the fun we've been having; however, I think you're right; you have to show me much more of our wonderful World. Although, I hope we can come back at some time and visit. Will you tell Lewis?'

That night, the Emperors stood along the ice edge with Zak and I floating alongside the ice shelf. We chatted to each other under a blue, black sky full of thousands of bright twinkling stars. With the full moon, it was almost like daylight with the moon's reflection on the ice.

When there was a lull in our conversation Zak told Lewis our plan to move on. Lewis smiled and said, 'Zak, we always knew that you and Rory were only here for a visit, and to help us. It would be too cold for you to stay. However, before you go could you tell us one of your stories?'

I looked at Zak, surprised. 'Zak I didn't know you were a storyteller!'

Before Zak could respond, Lewis spoke. 'Rory, Zak has been entertaining us with his stories for years. It's one of the things we look forward to when we see him. Come on Zak tell us a story.'

Zak smiled then said. 'OK give me a few minutes while I think of one.'

While Zak was thinking the Emperors gathered in a tight group round on the ice edge and in the water surrounding Zak and some were even lying on his back, they all wanted to hear Zak's story. Zak gave a deep rumble and cleared his throat, which sent tremors of vibrations through the water, then he spoke.

Chapter 6

'This story starts hundreds of years ago when we hardly ever saw humans and when we did, they sailed on small ships with sails, which glided them across the water. They didn't interfere with our way of life and generally left us alone. They did however attack each other with things they called cannons which fired big round metal balls and gave off lots of smoke when they were fired. The worst area for fighting seemed to be around the area known as the Caribbean.

The Caribbean has a mixture of small and large islands where the humans would anchor to rest or hide their ships. It was also part of the route the humans used to cross, sailing between what they call America and Europe.

There was one human and his ship who would attack all the ships they saw. He was called Black Bart Scar Face and he was called a pirate by the humans. He was a giant among humans, standing at more than two metres tall. He had jet black hair and a massive black beard. Everything about him was black, his clothes, even his teeth.

When he attacked other ships, he blacked his face with charcoal and had burning fuses tied in his beard that he used to help fire the cannon. He was a fearsome sight and terrified his enemies.

His crew of cut throats was equally terrifying, amongst them was his mate, Cutlass Jones who had lost half an ear and part of his nose in lots of sword fights.

Another of the crew was one-eyed Smelly Jane. A smelly woman who never washed and had long lank greasy hair. She had a seventy-five-millimetre scar down her face which she got from a sword fight, where she killed her opponent. She also lost sight in one eye, when a splinter of wood kicked up by a cannonball during a battle with another ship pierced her eye. She was as evil as the rest of the crew and she was just as deadly with a knife. No one would dare cross her, as she would wait until they were sleeping, then creep up, put her hand over their mouths then slit their throats.

Black Bart's ship was a galleon called the 'Devil's Revenge.' He had it painted in black. The only white on the ship was the figurehead, which was carved in wood, in the shape of a three-metre tall skeleton. The bones of the skeleton were highlighted in pure white paint, with the eye sockets and mouth painted in bright red, with red paint running from the mouth down the chin like dripping blood. The ship had jet-black dyed sails. Black Bart had also run red paint down the sails to look like blood. At the top of each mast, he had impaled a bleached white grinning skull with red paint running down the chin.

The Devil's Revenge carried seventy cannons, spread over two decks, and could fight most of the ships at that time. He also flew the Jolly Rodger, the pirate's flag, from his topmost mast beside a grinning skull.

If any ships, including other pirate ships, saw the Devil's Revenge on the horizon they tried to get away as quick as they could. The crew never washed, and you could smell the ship from hundreds of metres away.

Black Bart and his crew may never have washed, but he was a good sailor and he looked after his ship. Every year he would run the ship onto a beach in a secret cove. Then the crew would scrape and clean the keel, taking off barnacles and anything that was attached that could slow the ship down. They would rub and tar the ship's timbered keel, sew and repair the sails and do any maintenance that would help make the ship as fast as it could be.

Black Bart also had a paid network of spies around the Caribbean, who used a small fleet of Caravels. The Caravels were small fast cargo ships that traded around the Caribbean. The Caravels looked out for Galleons and ships loaded with riches, then informed Black Bart of the route that the richest and slowest ships would take, so he could mount an attack. Caravels would also pick up messages from Black Bart's spies and pass them on to Black Bart.

Chapter 7

The Spanish Main had been under the control of Spain since a famous Spanish explorer called Christopher Columbus landed in the Caribbean in 1492. The King of Spain appointed a Governor to oversee the area covering the north coast of South America, Central America, the Caribbean, and the western shore of The Gulf of Mexico. Central America was also an overland bridge for goods that the Spanish Galleons brought from China via Manila in the Philippines across the Pacific Ocean to Acapulco. The Galleons would unload their goods at Acapulco, the goods would then be carried across the land by carts and donkeys to the Caribbean Coast and onto Veracruz then finally loaded onto Galleons bound for Spain. Added to the treasures of gold and silver gathered in the Spanish Main were the goods from China and pieces of eight from Bolivia.

As the Spanish King's representative, the Governor was the most powerful person in the area. He had complete authority and only answered to the King.

One of the Governors was called Francisco Martinez de Baeza who had taken up his appointment as a young married man. The Governor and his wife had two children while in the Caribbean, a son, Juan, and daughter Isabella. When they reached school age the Governor and his wife decided that the mother would take the children to Spain to be educated. For safety, they planned their trip on board The San Miguel, which was the fastest Spanish Galleon in the Caribbean, and carried treasure for the King.

The San Miguel had crossed the Caribbean to Spain many times and outran any pirate ship she had seen. This was down to the speed of the Galleon and the seamanship of the captain.

As the San Miguel was being loaded with the treasure and supplies for its journey, one of Black Bart's spies was sitting on a capstan in the harbour smoking his clay pipe. He wore a Tricorn hat which kept his eyes shaded so he could watch the activity along the quay without drawing attention to himself. As he watched he counted the amount of treasure and provisions going on board. Sitting on the capstan at the edge of the quay he could also see how far the Galleon was settling in the water as it was loaded.

When the Governor arrived with his wife and children to board, it was obvious from their luggage that they were going to travel with San Miguel and the treasure to Spain. The spy almost bit through his pipe in excitement, he had to get away and get a message to Black Bart, this would be a Galleon he would love to capture.

The spy stood up looked around. He slowly tapped his pipe against the capstan, put it in his pocket then quickly walked through the harbour, past the warehouses full of goods to where his horse was tied. He couldn't wait to send his message to Black Bart. If Black Bart captured the Galleon and the governor's wife and children, he would be paid a fortune. He mounted and quickly rode, hanging tightly onto his hat, to a headland point ten kilometres away, to send smoke signals.

Out at sea one of Black Bart's Caravels picked up the message. Realising the importance of the message it turned away from shore sailing off as fast as it could, to rendezvous with Black Bart and 'The Devil's Revenge.' This could be a massive treasure for Black Bart and his crew if they could capture the treasure Galleon. They would have the treasure, capture the Governor's wife and children and hold them for ransom. The Governor would pay a fortune to get his family back and might even pardon some of Black Bart's crew who had been captured and were languishing in jail.

Chapter 8

Normally the treasure Galleons would muster at Havana in Cuba, then sail across the Atlantic Ocean in convoy for protection. However, the Governor and the San Miguel's Captain decided that they would bypass Cuba and sail directly to Spain, hopefully surprising any pirates and their spies, who would expect them to go to Cuba and wait there.

The San Miguel had four masts, weighed seven hundred tons, and had two decks, with a total of fifty cannons. Normally it would have had a crew of three hundred sailors, however, to give the governor's wife and children space the crew had been reduced to two hundred and fifty sailors.

They sailed with good winds blowing, so the Captain unfurled all the sails for maximum speed. He wanted to get to Spain as quickly as he could, to safely deliver his passengers and treasure.

The family soon settled into a routine on board, with the children having some lessons, but also a lot of free time. On the third day at sea, the children were at the bow of the San Miguel looking out when a pod of dolphins exploded out of the water and rode the bow wave of the Galleon.

The children were mesmerised watching the dolphins twisting, turning, surfing, and flipping on the waves. The children could hear the dolphins chattering to each other, it was as if they were boasting about the tricks they could do and how high they could reach.

The children started to identify individual dolphins and gave them names. One was called Jack, as they thought it was like a Jack in the Box, suddenly exploding out of the water then rising high in the air. Another one was called Lightning, as it appeared to be the fastest of the dolphins and was like a silver streak powering through the water. There was also The Joker, as this dolphin always seemed to be laughing and chattering to the other dolphins. Four young dolphins in the group tried to copy the adult dolphins.

Every day after lessons the children would rush to the bow of the San Miguel to look for the dolphins. After three days the dolphins seem to recognise the children. At one point, Jack rose out of the water, and up the side of the San Miguel so high that he looked down on the children. As he did, he let out what seemed to be a laugh then what appeared to be a wink, twisted then dived back into the water. The children stood stunned. After a few minutes, they ran to tell their mother.

Their mother listened to their story, then went with them to the bow to have a look. There, exactly as the children had said, were the dolphins riding the bow waves. As they watched the children pointed out the different dolphins by their names. The mother, like the children, was

enthralled by the dolphins.

After watching for an hour, the mother said to the children, 'Go and ask the cook if he can spare some dried fish. If he has, we could feed them to the dolphins.'

The children ran off as fast as they could down the deck to find the cook.

After ten minutes the children came back with a small bucket filled with fish. They took the bucket to the bow of the Galleon, picked out a fish each, and waited for the dolphins. After ten minutes the dolphins appeared and exploded out of the water. The children watched and waited for the right moment to throw their fish. As usual, Jack was first to jump. As he jumped one of the children threw their fish. Jack was caught by surprise. He didn't expect to have fish thrown at him. However, with quick responses, he twisted and dived after the fish and caught it before it hit the water.

The rest of the dolphins quickly realised what was happening and jumped out of the water performing tricks and catching the fish. When the crew saw what was happening, they watched from the decks and the rigging of the Galleon and started cheering and clapping at the dolphin's tricks. Later that day over their dinner everyone was talking and telling stories about the dolphins.

Chapter 9

All was well on board the San Miguel. However, the spy's Caravel made good speed carrying his message and after two days caught up with Black Bart and the Devils Revenge. Black Bart listened to the message sitting in his stateroom. As he listened his black tooth grin got bigger and bigger. He clapped his hands and tugged at his beard in excitement then rose and shouted for Jane to get the crew together.

As he strode out onto the deck the crew gathered in silence, they watched the Caravel come alongside and the messenger going with Black Bart into the stateroom. They knew from previous messengers that there must be a treasure ship around to be attacked and they could have more money. Black Bart stood grinning as the crew waited for the news.

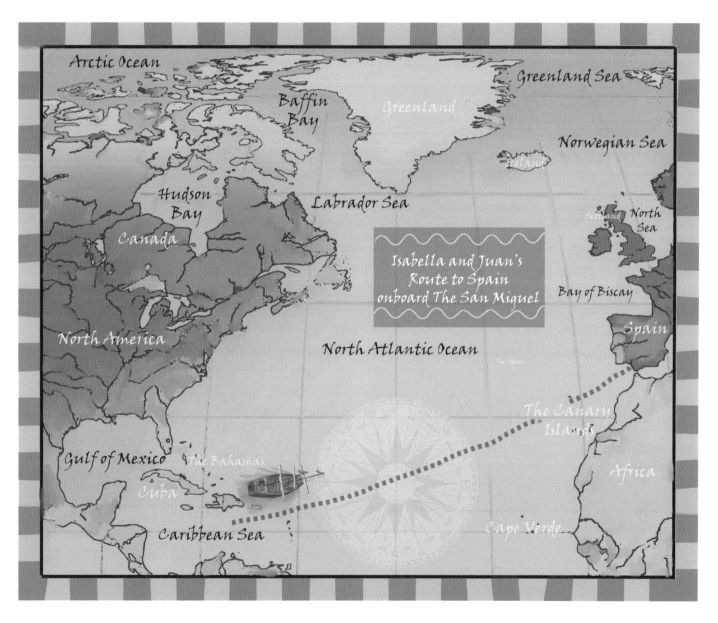

'RIGHT! me mateys,' said Bart. 'I've just had news that the biggest treasure ever to be seen, is on our patch of sea. It's loaded with Spanish Treasure but even better, the Governor's wife and children are also on board. If we can capture them, the Governor will pay enough money to get his family back for all of us to retire rich. He would even ask the King of Spain for money to get his family back. We need to capture the San Miguel.

Listening to some of the crew of the treasure Galleon at the inn before sailing, our spies have found out that they are not going to Cuba but sailing alone straight across the Atlantic without stopping. I've sent the Caravel crew to search to the North and if they see any of our Caravels to form a chain twenty kilometres apart. If they spot the Galleon they will send us a message using a series of flares.'

With an evil grin and rubbing his hands, Black Bart said, 'Capturing the San Miguel and its treasure along with the Governor's family, is going to make us the richest pirates in the world, never mind the Caribbean. RIGHT! ME MATEYS, let's get this ship ready for action! Remember we'll need to get in close, as we don't want to sink her and lose the treasure.'

The pirate ship became a hive of activity as the crew set every sail that the Devils Revenge carried. The lookouts climbed to the highest mast and sat beside the skulls, scanning the horizon with their telescopes searching for the treasure Galleon. While the gun crew checked the cannons, the boarding crew checked their muskets, sharpened their cutlasses and daggers. The whole ship was buzzing with excitement as the crew thought about the riches they could capture. They couldn't wait to get into action.

Chapter 10

Onboard the San Miguel life had settled into a routine of lessons, meals, and the highlight of the day, feeding and watching the dolphins. The dolphins arrived at the same time every day, they knew when the children would throw food for them. Everything seemed perfect, the weather was good with the winds filling the sails and driving the San Miguel on. Even the Captain and senior officers were reasonably relaxed although they wouldn't totally relax until they saw the coast of Spain.

One afternoon the children were on deck after their lessons ready to feed the dolphins but there was no sign of them. The children peered over the side then up to the bow of the Galleon where the dolphins normally rode the waves but there were no dolphins. For an hour they walked from side to side then up to the bow of the Galleon but still no sign. Despondently the children walked back to their mother's cabin. As soon as they walked in, she knew something was wrong.

'What's wrong with you two?' she asked.

'Our dolphins have gone!' they said in unison. 'We've been looking for them for over an hour with fish scraps, but they're not there,' Isabella continued.

The mother smiled, put her arms around them then said, 'Come on, let's go on deck and have another look.'

They left the cabin and walked onto the deck. The sun was shining on the sea so they could see for several kilometres around the San Miguel, but there was no sign or sighting of anything, not even the dolphins.

The Captain had watched them come onto the deck and look out to the sea around the Galleon. He left the bridge and walked down the deck to the trio to ask what they were looking for. When they told him, he pushed his Captain's hat back on his head and scratched his exposed head. He appeared perplexed and deep in thought before he spoke.

'You know I think something's wrong, in all my years of being at sea you always see something about your vessel. It could be dolphins, fish jumping or if you're really, lucky, a whale or a school of whales. When there appears to be nothing around it usually means a storm's brewing. Our barometer is set fair, and all the signs are that the weather is to stay good. We'll have to keep our sailor's weather eye on the conditions and watch for any changes. I'm sure your dolphins will be back tomorrow, after all they've been getting a free meal. They'll be back.'

Galileo's Barometer

The Compass Rose

Astrolabe

And with that, he pulled his cap back onto his head, looked around then headed back to the bridge. He was troubled but didn't want to alarm his passengers. He sent a member of the crew to the topmast with a telescope, gathered the senior officers, and checked the instruments. He ordered the officers to be extra vigilant as there was an eeriness surrounding the Galleon, he didn't know what it was, but he had a feeling something was wrong and something bad was going to happen.

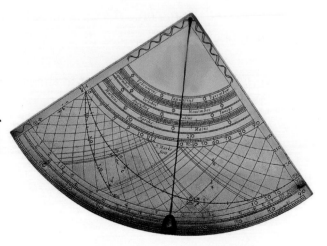

Mariner's Quadrant

Chapter 11

The Captain was right to be concerned. Sitting low on the horizon unsighted by the San Miguel, one of Black Bart's Caravels had seen them. The Caravel slowly turned away from the San Miguel so it would not be seen. Then, when it was out of sight, unfurled its sail and headed off in the direction of the Devil's Revenge. The dolphins had sensed the faster Caravel and had headed off to ride the faster waves. The dolphins followed the caravel all the way to the Devil's Revenge.

The Captain of the Caravel gave Black Bart the news, the location of the San Miguel and how far it was from The Devil's Revenge. Black Bart did two things. He sent the Caravel to spread the news and to bring back all the Caravels. He then readied the crew to sail the Devils Revenge as fast as they could in pursuit of the San Miguel. The boarding crew brought their weapons to the deck. Their cutlasses and daggers were like mirrors shining in the sun. They checked, cleaned and greased their muskets. When they saw the dolphins, they thought they would have some target practice.

Jack and the rest of the dolphins had kept a good distance away from the Devil's Revenge. Even the dolphins found the smell from the ship disgusting. They were circling around watching when the Caravel headed off. They were unsure whether to follow the Caravel or to head back to the San Miguel. As they watched, the Devil's Revenge ran out all its sails, rose in the water as the wind filled its sails, creating a big bow wave, then headed in the direction of the San Miguel.

Jack and the dolphins realised that the Devil's Revenge was heading towards the San Miguel and decided to ride its bow waves. Onboard the Devil's Revenge, the boarding crew had loaded their muskets and were watching the dolphins. They knew the dolphins wouldn't be able to resist riding the bow wave. The boarding crew positioned themselves at the bow and waited.

Jack and the Joker rose out of the water ahead of the rest of the pod when there was a noise like thunder. Jack felt something tear through his dorsal fin and fell back into the water. The Joker felt something tear across his nose and leave a furrow on his skin, he also fell back into the water. The rest of the pod quickly dived under the water and headed away from the Devil's Revenge. The dolphins gathered away from the ship and checked Jack's and the Joker's wounds. Jack had three musket holes through his fin while the Joker had a tear across his nose where the musket ball had hit him. Onboard the Devil's Revenge the crew were cheering.

The dolphins followed the Devil's Revenge from a distance. Every so often one of the crew would fire their musket in the direction of the dolphins. The musket ball would fall harmlessly into the sea with a plop. The dolphins knew to keep out of range. As the dolphins followed, they realised that the Devil's Revenge was heading in the direction of the San Miguel. They would have to do something. These bad, smelly humans must be after the nice people on the San Miguel. But what could they do? They circled the Devil's Revenge out of range of the muskets chattering amongst themselves about what to do when they heard CLICK, CLICK, CLICK, CLICK through the water. The dolphins stopped and listened again. There it was. More clicks. They chattered and whistled to each other, then, Lightning took off as fast as he could travel in the direction of the clicks.

After thirty minutes Lightning came across a family school of Sperm whales. Lightning and his pod of dolphins was known to the school, in fact, the dolphins would play with the young whales. They would chase each other through leaps, dives, and twist and when they were tired, they would lie on the surface clicking and chattering to each other.

When Ruth the matriarch saw Lightning, she knew something was wrong, Lightning would never travel without the rest of his pod. The school gathered round while Lightning told his story. Lightning told them about the family and crew on the San Miguel, how friendly they were, and how they threw them scraps of fish to eat when they were riding the waves. Lightning's tone changed when he talked about Black Bart and The Devil's Revenge. He explained the pirates had shot their muskets injuring Jack and The Joker. Ruth and the school listened but were stunned when Lightning asked Ruth to help them stop the pirates from chasing their friends.

Ruth shook her giant head slowly then spoke to Lightning with the school listening. 'We know about Black Bart and his pirates. We also know to keep far away from The Devil's Revenge, because as soon as we get within range of its cannons, they fire at us. The cannonballs fall into the sea, but we understand about not getting too close. I don't know what we could do to help, we don't want to be shot at by their cannon.'

Lightning grinned, 'We know all that, but we have a plan which would surprise the pirates and could only be carried out by whales. You would be our secret weapon working with us. The key to it is timing, our pod of dolphins could get in close enough to give the signal for your school's adults to surprise the pirates. Do you want to know our plan?'

Ruth looked at the adults in the school who were nodding their heads up in agreement. 'Right' Ruth said, 'It looks like you've got a secret weapon, what's your plan?'

The adult whales gathered around as Lightning outlined his plan. When he finished the whole school was waving their flukes up and down clapping. Ruth organised the school, the young adults would look after the calves and take them away from danger. She then gathered the adults to run through the plan one more time.

While Ruth was doing this Lightning headed back to his pod who were shadowing the Devil's Revenge.

Chapter 12

Onboard the Devil's Revenge, Black Bart was pacing impatiently up and down the deck. He had blackened his face and laced the cannon fuses through his beard. He was ready for action. He desperately wanted to see the San Miguel. He wanted the treasure and the Governor's family as hostages. Every ten minutes he would shout at the lookouts for a sighting, when they shouted back that there was nothing, Black Bart disappointed and in a rage would punch or kick anyone nearby. The crew learned to keep out of his way.

The dolphins slowly circled the Devil's Revenge staying low in the water and out of range of the muskets. Unknown to them they were safe. While the crew and Black Bart had noticed them, the San Miguel was the only thing they wanted.

Just before dusk one of the lookouts caught a speck of white on the horizon and shouted 'SAIL HO, SHIP AHOY!' and pointed in the direction of the sail.

On deck Black Bart ran to the bridge, grabbed his compass and took a bearing using the direction the lookout was pointing. Black Bart's lips pulled back to a grin exposing his black teeth. He would have his treasure tomorrow.

He gathered his crew together to give them their instructions. 'RIGHT! Me shipmates, tonight we will all rest and eat. We'll keep our sails unfurled, to keep up this speed, but I don't want to go any faster in case we sail past them in the dark. Make sure your weapons are ready, because we'll catch them easy enough tomorrow, then we'll all be the richest pirates in the world. No drinking tonight, I want you all sober tomorrow, but when we capture the treasure, we'll have a big party.'

While the pirates were sailing through the night Ruth and her whales had met Lightning and the dolphins near the San Miguel. As they knew Black Bart was after the San Miguel the first part of the plan was to wait close by for the Devil's Revenge to appear. They could feel the vibrations and the noise of the Devil's Revenge through the water as it sailed towards the San Miguel.

At dawn the next morning the Devil's Revenge was in sight of the San Miguel. As night's darkness rolled over the horizon and the dawn became brighter the San Miguel's lookout gasped in surprise. He saw a massive black ship with black sails topped with the skull and crossbones. The Devil's Revenge was sailing straight towards them! He shouted a warning down below. On the deck, everyone rushed to the rail to see for themselves.

What they saw sent shivers down their spines. The Devil's Revenge and Black Bart! Laden and weighed down with treasure, there was no way they could outrun the Devil's Revenge.

The Governor's wife ran to the Captain who was on the bridge.

'Well Captain what do you intend to do?'

The Captain shrugged his shoulders. He opened his hand's palm outwards and said, 'What can I do? We can't outrun Black Bart and we can't outgun him. His ship is too fast and powerful.'

'Captain,' the governor's wife said, 'You will do everything you can to evade him. There is always a chance something might happen that lets us escape. We could sail into a Spanish convoy, even the British or Dutch would be better than that monster. We are not going to give in without trying to escape and, if need be, to fight. Give me and my children weapons. They have been trained in firing pistols and muskets and my son is good with a sword. We will help you fight if necessary. But I'm not giving in to a pirate without a fight. Do everything you can to save us and your San Miguel.'

With that, she walked off leaving the Captain looking at the Devil's Revenge and wondering what to do. He looked at the sails - there were no more he could raise. The San Miguel was sailing as fast as possible. He thought about throwing the treasure overboard, but he knew if they were captured Black Bart would fly into a rage. His temper and rages were infamous and there were many stories about what he had done in anger. All the San Miguel's Captain could do was pray and stay as far in front of the Devil's Revenge as he could. Perhaps if they got through the day and made it to the night, they might lose the pirates in the dark.

Chapter 13

Onboard the Devil's Revenge, Black Bart mustered his crew and with an excited voice gave them their orders.

'RIGHT! ME MATEYS! Gun crews open your gun hatches and run out your cannons. When you are in range, I want you to fire shots in front of, behind, and to the side of the San Miguel. I don't want a single shot to hit the Galleon, I want to take it intact. If anyone fires a shot that hits the San Miguel, I'll get Smelly Jane to give twenty lashes to each of the gun crew that fired the shot. OK, gun crew carry out your orders. Right the rest of you, scurvy bunch. Open all the deck hatches to let the smoke out from the cannons, check your weapons and I want the best marksmen in the rigging, so, if you get a clear sight of the crew on the San Miguel you can fire. Remember we want the governor's wife and children unhurt so be careful with your shot or you'll have Smelly Jane to answer to.'

All morning the Devil's Revenge slowly closed in on the Galleon. At one point the San Miguel's Captain thought he was matching the same speed as the Devils Revenge and there may be a chance of staying out of range till nightfall. That all changed in the early afternoon. The Devil's Revenge was within range to fire her cannons.

The first shot whistled through the air and fell into the sea raising a giant water plume in front of the San Miguel. It was followed by a thunderous noise as the rest of the cannon opened fire. The San Miguel was surrounded by giant fountains of water as the cannonballs landed in the sea. There was a loud cheer from the Devil's Revenge which carried all the way across the water.

Onboard the San Miguel everyone stood wide-eyed and shaking in fear, with white ashen faces. The Devil's Revenge had the San Miguel in range and could disable it or sink it at any time. They felt how a mouse must feel when being chased and cornered by a cat. Everything that happened next was in the hands of the pirates. All they could do was wait.

Onboard the Devil's Revenge Black Bart ordered the gun crews to fire another broadside. Perhaps this would make the San Miguel Captain realise there was no chance of escape. The gun crews were deadly accurate, and their cannonballs landed in the same pattern as the first salvo.

On the San Miguel the Captain went to the Governor's wife and said they should surrender before they were sunk.

The governor's wife explained to the Captain. 'Captain we will never surrender as long as we are afloat, we will keep fighting. Have I made myself clear? I do not want my children in that monster's clutches. Keep sailing and do your best to stay in front.'

The gap between the ships slowly closed. In the afternoon the wind dropped and both ships drifted to a stop. The San Miguel's Captain was first to react. He quickly lowered two longboats and crews who rowed to the front of the Galleon. When they were in position the crew onboard threw them long ropes which were tied to the rear of the longboats and the bow of the San Miguel. With the ropes secured the oarsmen on the longboat dug their oars deep into the water and pulled. Both longboat oarsmen pulled in unison and the San Miguel slowly started to move and pull away from the Devil's Revenge and Black Bart.

Onboard the Devil's Revenge Black Bart saw what was happening and ordered a gun crew to fire on the longboats. The first cannon fired however, as the speed of the San Miguel had increased the cannonball flew through one of the San Miguel's sails.

Black Bart was incandescent with rage and shouted, 'Ceasefire! Jane, get down and sort out that gun crew.'

He paced up and down the deck and onto the bridge fuming and looking towards the San Miguel. His ship was too big to tow with longboats, but he wanted the San Miguel.

Suddenly he stopped and grinned, he shouted up to the lookouts, 'Can you see the Caravel?' 'Aye Captain,' was the reply, 'She's coming up astern.'

Black Bart clapped his hands. He had a plan which would stop the San Miguel.

When the Caravel caught up with The Devil's Revenge the Captain was ordered on board by Black Bart to receive orders. As the Caravel was lighter, they were to use what wind there was, sail and row the Caravel across and sink the longboats towing the San Miguel. Black Bart added some of his own crew to help the Caravel row.

Onboard the San Miguel they watched as the Caravel left and headed off in their direction towards the longboats. However, the San Miguel Captain was an experienced sailor and knew what they planned. As the Caravel drew closer it came within range of the San Miguel's cannons. The Captain readied his gun crews then waited hidden behind closed gun ports. Onboard the Caravel the crew raised their muskets to fire on the longboat crews when there was an enormous explosion. The San Miguel was covered in smoke from its cannons, which had fired at point-blank range on the Caravel. The crew had dropped the gun port catching the caravel by surprise. When the smoke cleared all that was left of the Caravel were bits of floating wood and sail with pirates hanging on.

When Black Bart saw what happened he stormed up and down the deck kicking out at anything or anyone that got in his way.

Over the next few hours, the gap between the two ships grew, however, Black Bart had calmed down, he knew the winds would change and he would finally capture San Miguel. Every hour on the San Miguel the Captain changed the rowing crews on the longboats. The rowers rowed one hour in every three. They never complained because they knew their lives depended on getting away from Black Bart. As darkness fell the gap between the two ships had increased. The San Miguel out was out of range of the Devil's Revenge's cannons.

All through the night, the rowers rowed, hoping their efforts would get them further and further away from Black Bart. The captain of the San Miguel ordered no lights to be lit and the no one should speak. If they had to, only in a whisper. He didn't want to give the pirates a clue where they were in the darkness.

As the first light of dawn broke both crews looked out to check the position of the other ship. The Devil's Revenge was still in sight, but a gap had opened between them during the night.

The crew on the San Miguel were having a well-earned breakfast when they heard a loud clap. They all looked at each other in silence, then threw their plates and breakfast aside. They knew what that clap was. On deck, the sails were starting to fill and flap, the winds had arrived. The Captain quickly untied the ropes from the rowing boat and got the rowers and their boats back on board. He plotted a course towards the convoy lanes hoping to meet other ships before Black Bart caught up.

On the Devil's Revenge, the wind was slower to fill its sails and Black Bart watched as the San Miguel sailed further away. However, as the winds grew in strength the Devil's Revenge's sails puffed out and drove the ship on after the San Miguel.

Onboard the San Miguel the initial excitement wore off as they saw the sails of the Devil's Revenge's fill with wind and the bow wave rise as she gave chase.

As the chase restarted unknown to the sailors, Ruth, the whales and dolphins were watching from a distance. They watched as the gap closed between the two ships and when the Devil's Revenge started firing on the San Miguel they knew they would have to put their plan into action.

Black Bart was determined not to let the San Miguel escape again, and as he closed the gap, he ordered his gun crews to keep up the bombardment around the San Miguel so that when he moved the Devil's Revenge alongside the San Miguel close enough to board, the San Miguel would hopefully surrender. The Devil's Revenge was shrouded in smoke from the cannons which was pouring out of the gun ports and the open deck hatches. Black Bart's lookouts were shouting down directions as they were above the smoke and could guide the Devil's Revenge towards the San Miguel.

In the distance slowly swimming on the surface, the dolphins were watching the ships close the gap. When the gap had nearly closed there was a series of chatters and clicks transmitted through the water. The dolphins were sending messages to Ruth and the rest of the whales who were deep under the water below the Devil's Revenge. Finally, the message was sent to the whales, now was the time for the whales to attack Black Bart and the Devil's Revenge.

As the gap closed Black Bart lit the fuses in his beard, he was going into battle and wanted to scare the San Miguel crew. Suddenly Black Bart was swept off his feet by a cascade of water and his fuses were extinguished. He tried to rise back to his feet, however, the wave knocked him over again. This time he swallowed a mouthful of salty seawater. He knelt, doubled up, and coughed on the deck. What was going on? Where was the water coming from?

Onboard the San Miguel they readied themselves as the Devil's Revenge closed the gap. They knew Black Bart would try to board them to take their ship intact. As they watched the Devil's Revenge, on either side of its hull, two fountains of water shot up and cascaded onto the deck of the pirate's ship. They stared in amazement as another two fountains shot up out of the sea and once again landed on the deck of the Devil's Revenge. This was quickly followed by another two. The Devil's Revenge was being sprayed with continuous fountains of water. The San Miguel Captain looked at the sky and sea for any signs of twisters or mini twisters, but everything was normal. The Captain looked again towards the Devil's Revenge, this time he caught a glimpse of a whale's fluke. He shook his head in confusion. Whales would normally avoid human contact. But there they were whales were running along both sides of the Devil's Revenge in a constant procession, spraying the decks with hundreds of litres of seawater.

Onboard his ship Black Bart tried to stand and walk across the deck to reach the deck rail. He wanted to see want was happening. He stumbled and swayed until he made it to the deck rail. He stared over to see a massive shape rise through the water towards his ship. Then suddenly he was hit with a fountain of saltwater which knocked him off his feet. As he sat dazed on the deck he looked around. Something was wrong he thought.

Meantime fountain after fountain of water was hitting the deck. After sitting for a few minutes, he groggily rose to his feet hanging on tightly to a deck rope. As he stood, he realised that the deck was tilting. What was going on? With alarm he knew what it was, all the deck and cannon covers were open to let the cannon smoke out when the gunners fired the cannon. That was letting the saltwater water run down into the ship. He had to close the hatches and cannon doors, or his ship would sink.

He tried shouting an order, but every time he opened his mouth to shout, he swallowed a mouth full of saltwater. All around him his crew was floundering on the deck. Every time they stood up, they got knocked down with the cascading water. Black Bart could feel his ship settling low in the water as it slowly filled up with water. Soon the gun crews emerged from the hatches, the water level had reached the cannon. They looked around at Black Bart wondering what was happening. As the Devil's Revenge settled further into the sea, the gun ports, which had been

opened to fire the cannon, let more water pour into the ship. Realising the Devil's Revenge was sinking, Black Bart gave the order to abandon the ship.

The pirates launched their longboats and climbed aboard, quickly rowing away from their fast, sinking ship. The ship sank lower and lower into the water until it gave out a last gasp and whoosh as the remaining air trapped inside found its way to the surface. The stern reared up then the Devil's Revenge started its last journey... to the bottom of the sea.

Onboard the San Miguel everyone had been watching in amazement, as the whales sprayed the Devil's Revenge. As Black Bart and the pirates slowly rowed away in their longboats the whales circled the San Miguel. Suddenly everyone on the San Miguel was terrified, they had seen what they had done to The Devil's Revenge. The Captain quickly gave the order to close all hatches while everyone braced themselves for a deluge of water. Nothing happened, the whales slowly circled round the Galleon. Suddenly there were flashes of silver around the whales.

The children were first to understand and shouted out. 'Jack, Joker, Lightning! That's our dolphins!'

Suddenly everyone on board was dancing, clapping, and cheering the dolphins and whales. The whales and dolphins cavorted around the Galleon for over an hour. Leaping and twisting out of the water, the dolphins leaping over the whales' backs, entertaining the humans then suddenly they dived under the water and disappeared.

The San Miguel continued its journey safely to Spain where its rescue story was told. Of course, no one believed them, after all, how could whales sink a pirate's ship?

Juan the Governor's son went to school and university in Madrid. When he finished his education the King of Spain made him Governor of a new Spanish colony, California.

When Zak finished his story there was complete silence, they were all enthralled. Suddenly there was a crescendo of noise, the Emperors were flapping their wings against each other and stamping their feet on the ice. They were all cheering Zak.

Lewis spoke first, 'Zak, fantastic, another brilliant story. It was just a story, wasn't it?'

Zak just smiled and said nothing. I looked at Zak, I was puzzled, 'Zak I don't understand how the whales could make the water fountains. When you surface you blow any water that's sitting on your blowhole away so you can breathe, but it's not a fountain, more a mist.'

Zak smiled at me, 'It's a trick we learn as calves. If we blow out three to four metres under the water as we surface, we produce a big fountain. It takes a bit of practice but once you get the hang of it's a good trick.'

'What happened to the pirates?'

Zak looked to see who had asked the question. It was Susan who was standing with her chick. Zak smiled and winked at Susan's chick before he replied.

'In whale folklore, there are stories of a black ghost ship with black sails and what appears to be red blood running down the sails with a skeleton as a figurehead. It's manned by a crew of skeletons who stare from red eye sockets straight ahead. It appears from nowhere. Generally, out of the sea mist, then disappears.

There is a story of a whale seeing it on a clear night bearing straight down on a sailing ship. The sailing ship's crew were so terrified they were being rammed they left everything behind including their dinner, then jumped overboard. They watched as the ghost ship appear to hit then pass through their ship. Their ship was unharmed, and the ghost ship sailed on. Unfortunately for the crew in the water, their ship was under sail, so it carried on without a crew and left them behind in the water, where they perished. The name of the ship was the Marie Celeste and humans are still trying to find out what happened to it, they call it a ghost ship. But we know it's not, we know what happened.'

We spent the rest of the night looking at the stars, chatting and telling stories. The next morning Zak and I left the Emperors. We were both sad to be leaving but happy to be renewing our travels. As we headed off there was a massive last colourful Mexican wave from the Emperors. When we were out of sight, I asked Zak where we were going.

He replied, 'Let's head back to the Atlantic to see if we can meet any of our friends and my family.'

With that, we headed towards the Atlantic Ocean looking for new and old friends and adventures.

Chapter 14

Zak and I were swimming slowly Northwards chatting when we noticed a large, leathery, inky-black shell heading towards us. Zak looked at me, then stared at the shell giving it a long look. Then he let out a laugh.

'Rory it's Rog, he's paddling as fast as he can and heading straight for us.'

I was surprised and excited. Rog, or Rodger giving him his full name, was a Leatherback Turtle that we both knew and had had an adventure with before. As the shell drew near Rog angled and stretched his head out of his shell above the waves and shouted.

'Hi Zak, Hi Rory I'm glad I've found you. I've got some bad news.'

Zak and I slowed down and waited for Rog to join us. When Rog caught up, we exchanged pleasantries then Rog became serious giving Zak a hard stare.

'Zak the whalers are back, they've been searching looking for whales to hunt and kill. I don't think you should go any further North, that's where they are. You should turn and go back or head another way.'

Rog and I looked at Zak, we knew Zak's mother had been killed by whalers and Zak had been harpooned, requiring me to remove the harpoon. I had managed to disable the whaler's ship, enabling Zak and I to escape.

Zak shook his head, 'I don't know what to do. Every time we stop them, they come back, I just don't know what to do!' Zak was really distressed.

Rog and I were surprised to see how distressed Zak was, after all, sperm whales are one of the biggest and cleverest creatures in the oceans. To see Zak distressed upset us.

I looked at Zak, then thought hard and long and said, 'Zak I have a plan. It would mean taking on the whalers, and we would need assistance. What do you think?'

'Rory,' Zak replied, 'I'll try anything to stop the whalers, what's your plan?'

I outlined my plan to Zak and Rog. When I finished Zak smiled and turned to Rodger, 'What do you think Rog, would it work?'

Rodger thought for a moment, smiled, then replied, 'I think it's a good plan and could work, but it would need a lot of support and good timing. I think it's worth a try, but Zak, you need to get the resources.'

Zak smiled, 'You know I think with the right resources it could work. I'll get the resources.'

With that Zak let out a series of clicks that could travel many kilometres through the ocean, this is the way whales communicate with each other and other pods.

Zak turned to Rog, 'Right Rog, take us in the direction of the whalers so we can see what we are up against and if the plan would work.'

With that, we headed up the Atlantic towards the whalers, and hopefully the extra resources that Zak had called for through his clicks.

Chapter 15

After leading us North for two days Rog slowed down then stopped.

'Zak do you remember how to make me fly? I would like to look ahead, I don't think we are too far away now, could you launch me?'

This was a trick Zak and I had developed with Rog and used it while playing with the Emperor penguins in the Antarctic. It involved Rog positioning himself over Zak's giant fluke. When Rog was in position Zak would power his fluke upwards launching Rog out of the water then high into the air.

Rog positioned himself over Zak's fluke and shouted he was ready, then with a mighty whoosh and a cascade of water Rog flew up. As he flew, we could see him flapping his fins to guide his direction. When he reached the apex of his flight he glided back into the water with a gentle splash. He surfaced then swam over to join us.

'Wow, I'd forgotten how good it was to fly. I could see the whaler's boat far out on the horizon, it looks like they're just drifting slowly waiting for something to happen.'

'RIGHT' said Zak, 'Let's make it happen,' and he let out another series of clicks.

We lay drifting on the surface of the water for several hours, eventually, Rog asked Zak, 'Are you sure your message was received?'

He had just finished asking his question when two heads popped out of the water. 'Sam! Sue!' Zak shouted, 'you came!'

'Of course we came,' replied Sue, 'when we heard your message through the clicks. We hoped that you had a plan to sort out the whalers.'

Sam and Sue were Blue whales, as they were talking another four Blue whale heads appeared on the surface. You could see everyone was excited as they were all trying to talk and ask questions when another eight whales appeared. A small pod of Southern Right whales, led by Charlotte, joined in.

Zak, Rog, and I smiled at each other then I whispered to Zak, 'I didn't think you could get as many whales as this.'

Zak looked over his shoulder smiled and said, 'We're not finished, if you turn around, you'll see your old friend and his gang are here to join the fun.'

I turned slowly to see who Zak was talking about. There floating on the surface, with big wide grins, was Spike and his gang of Orcas. I rose out of the water, clapped my front flippers in excitement then made my way through the mass of whales to Spike.

'Hi Spike!' I shouted, 'I'm surprised to see you, I didn't think the whalers hunted Orcas.'

'Hi Rory!' the Orcas shouted in unison.

Spike was still grinning when he replied. 'As soon as we heard Zak's message, we knew we had to get here as quick as we could. If you pair are planning something, it's going to be good fun and we want to join in. Can you include us in your plan?'

I just smiled, mulled over what Spike had said, then replied, 'Spike, gang, we can use all the support we can get, you're in the plan.'

Chapter 16

As I had been speaking to Spike a massive white Sperm whale along with more Blue and Southern whales had arrived. Zak and Rog were going around talking to them, they were all asking the same question.

'Now we're here what's the plan?'

Zak slowly swam over to me with the white Sperm whale, 'Rory, I want you to meet my uncle George, he's come to join the party.'

I was puzzled George as was a white Sperm whale.

'Hello George,' I said 'it's a pleasure to meet you, when this is over could you tell me some stories about Zak? He doesn't give much away, and I would like to know more about him.'

George gave out a deep rumble chuckle then said, 'I'll be happy although, it would take too long to tell everything, but I'll tell you all the good and maybe some bad things.'

Zak smiled then spoke to the group, 'Hi Spike, Uncle George, I need to take Rory away, everyone wants to know what Rory's plan is.'

'No problem Zak, we also want to hear it, we want to see some action.'

Zak chuckled then replied, 'With Rory's plan you'll get some action! Come on Rory, time to tell everyone your plan.'

As we drifted towards the group I slowed and moved alongside Zak. Looking towards uncle George I whispered to Zak, 'Zak, why is your Uncle George white?'

Zak laughed, 'It's because he is quite old, sometimes Sperm whales turn white when they grow older. Come on let's tell everyone your plan.'

Zak shouted at everyone to gather. All the whales clustered around Zak while Rog and I climbed onto Zak's back to get a better view and all the whales could see me.

From Zak's back, it was an amazing sight, Blue whales, a white Sperm whale, Southern whales, Orcas, and there in the middle a giant Sperm whale with a Plesiosaur and a Leatherback turtle on its back. Humans wouldn't have believed the sight, all these creatures coming together and having a meeting. I looked at the sight with amazement, took a deep breath, then outlined my plan. There was total silence as I spoke. When I finished there were several seconds of silence, then one of the whales started beating its fluke up and down on the water. Suddenly all the whales were beating their flukes up and down, they were applauding my plan. Rog and I looked on in amazement, what a sight!

Zak shouted, 'Are you pair going to lounge about up there all day? Come on get down, it'll soon be night then we can put your plan into action.'

Rog and I looked at each other, then, counted one, two, three, then slid down Zak's back laughing as we splashed into the water.

'Right!' I shouted, 'you know the plan, you know what to do, you know the signal, let's go!'

With that, all the whales, Rog, and I slowly slipped below the surface and disappeared. Where there had been a mass of creatures, suddenly, the water was calm, with no ripples, no sight or trace of any creature. There was nothing to be seen from horizon to horizon, but under the water, a silent determined powerful army was swimming towards their enemy with a battle plan that required perfect co-ordination and power.

Onboard the whaler the crew were becoming restless. They only got paid if they killed whales. They had been at sea for four weeks looking for whales and hadn't seen any. They spent twenty-four hours a day manning their control room where they swept the surface with radar looking for any small blimp on the surface. They also had sonar which sent out underwater noise signals hoping to bounce off the whales but, to date, they had had no sight of any whales. During daylight hours they had crew members up in the highest masts with powerful binoculars searching the surface and horizon for any sign of whales.

That night the captain gathered most of the crew in the ship's mess. He wanted to tell them they were going to move to another search area as it was obvious there were no whales around. He left one member of the crew on the bridge to steer the ship and to look out for other shipping. If someone had been in the control room, they might have seen their controls and sonar going haywire. It appeared that there was a mass of large creatures surrounding the ship.

They were getting ready to put Rory's plan into action. Zak swam round the whaler checking all the whales, when he was ready, he gave three loud clicks.

Onboard the whaler the crew was listening to the captain, they were drinking tea, coffee, and sharing biscuits when they noticed the cups on the table were spilling over and the plates of biscuits were sliding across the tables. The captain shrugged his shoulders, the ship must have rolled in a small trough. He carried on talking to the crew.

The small movement that the captain felt was the whales getting into position. Under the ship, the Southern whales and Uncle George had positioned themselves along the keel of the ship. They were slowly raising the keel of the ship on their backs and lifting the whaler out of the water. On the other side, I was with Zak, the Blue whales, and Spike's gang. We positioned our heads along the side of the ship. On Zak's third click we pushed as hard as we could. As Uncle George and the Blue whales had been slowly lifting the ship out of the water, the ship started to slowly move sideways until it rested on the backs of the Southern Rights and Uncle George. Zak and his team kept pushing, while the Southern Rights and Uncle George angled their backs downwards, so the ship was out of the water and rolling down their backs sideways towards the water. Onboard the ship there were cries of alarm, the ship was rolling over and the crew was falling.

Zak and his team continued to push the ship down the Southern Rights backs and Uncle George's back until the ship was floating side-on in the water. When this happened, I and my army of sea creatures moved away from the ship, to watch what the whalers would do. As we watched the crew fell out of hatches and doorways that were above the water. They had life vests on and started freeing their life-boats and rafts. They piled into the rescue vessels, cut them from the ship then quickly paddled away from their ship. The ship slowly settled further in the water then suddenly let out a roar of air and hissing steam, then quickly sank, leaving only air bubbles and debris behind.

Chapter 17

The crew watched on in awe as their ship disappeared under the waves. They were in shock. What had happened? What caused their ship to sink? They looked around the ocean. There was nothing to see from horizon to horizon that could have sunk their ship. The ship's captain shouted to the lifeboats and life rafts to come together. He wanted to create a large floating raft to protect the sailors and to give them something to do.

The sailors busied themselves lining up the boats and rafts and securing them together. They were so busy that they had not noticed that the whale heads had slowly broken the surface surrounding their raft. The whales slowly moved towards the giant raft in an ever decreasing circle until they were only ten metres from the raft.

One of the sailors sensed something was watching. He stopped what he was doing, looked up, and out to sea. He looked straight at Zak with his giant head out of the water. The sailor tried to speak but all he managed was a croak, then he stumbled back and grabbed the nearest member of crew pointing at Zak. His crewmate looked where he was pointing, then fell back onto the raft in shock. By this time, the rest of the crew sensed something was wrong. They stopped what they were doing and looked out, they were shocked, amazed, and terrified, they were surrounded by whales and a monster.

This was part of my plan, I wanted to make the whalers so afraid they would never hunt whales again.

The whales slowly closed the circle around the sailors, then lay motionless staring at them. The sailors gathered in a huddle in the middle of their rafts frightened to move or talk. After three hours Zak let out a click, as the sailors watched the whales disappeared below the waves. At first, the sailors looked around numb with shock, then sat for several minutes in silence wondering where the whales had gone.

The first one to talk was the captain. As he started to speak there was an explosion of water around the raft. Suddenly the whales flew out of the water as high as they could then flipped in the air splashing back into the water creating a mini-wave that rocked the raft of crafts. The whalers shrank back in terror. They thought the whales were going to land on top of them. This was the final part of my plan. We all silently slid back under the water then rendezvoused three kilometres away.

We were all talking excitedly hoping that, perhaps, we had taught the whalers a lesson and perhaps they would think twice about hunting whales.

Sue came over to me. 'Rory' she said, 'It's been a pleasure to meet you and working together with the other whales to sort out the whalers. We had heard the rumours about a Plesiosaur, but we never thought we would ever meet one.'

I smiled at Sue and replied. 'I bet you heard the stories about a famous monster in Loch Ness in Scotland?'

'No' replied Sue. 'The rumours we heard were about a Plesiosaur off the Baja Peninsula.'

As we had been talking Zak swam over joining us. I looked at Zak then back to Sue then stuttered. ' B... B... Baja Peninsula? Where's that?'

'It's off the coast of Mexico in The Pacific Ocean,' she replied.

I lay back in the water stunned, trying to understand the implications of what Sue said. 'It means that there could be more Plesiosaurs!'

I looked back at Sue then shouted, 'COME ON ZAK! Take me to Baja!'

Zak joined in the excitement and shouted, 'Come on, let's go!'

With that, we waved goodbye to our smiling friends and headed off on our next journey. Heading for Baja, The Pacific Ocean, and hopefully to meet Plesiosaurs.

Pacific Centred Map

Showing Zak & Rory's Journey to the Baja Penisula

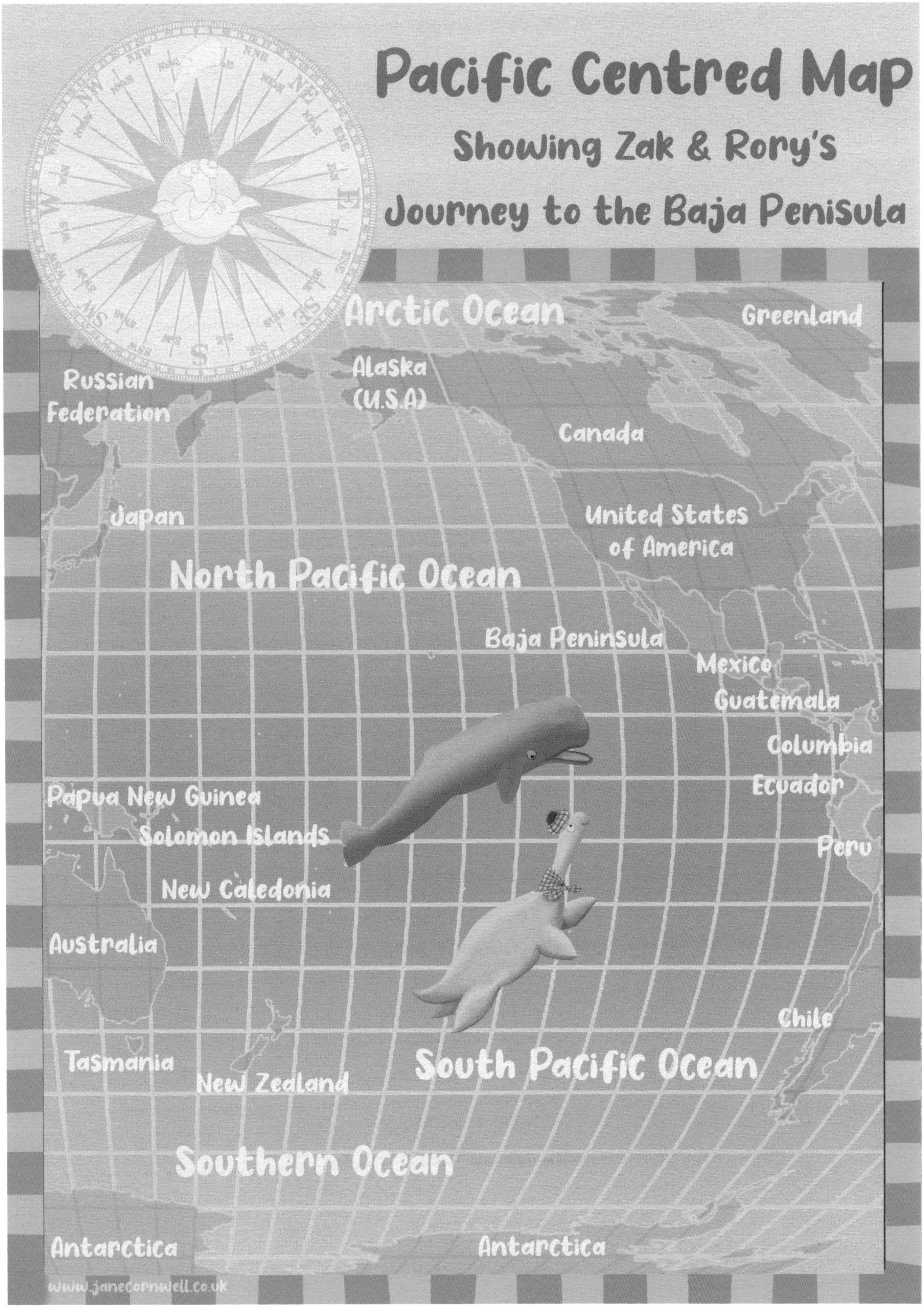

Arctic Ocean
Greenland
Russian Federation
Alaska (U.S.A)
Canada
Japan
United States of America
North Pacific Ocean
Baja Peninsula
Mexico
Guatemala
Columbia
Ecuador
Papua New Guinea
Solomon Islands
Peru
New Caledonia
Australia
Chile
Tasmania
New Zealand
South Pacific Ocean
Southern Ocean
Antarctica
Antarctica
www.janecornwell.co.uk

More Stories by Geoff Swift

The Friendly Giant Called Zak and His Friend
Rory the Misnamed Monster

Rory Never Learns:
A Mediterranean Sea Adventure
With Zak and Rory

Zak and Rory's Toughest Journey:
With Zak and Rory

The Witch, The Cat and Jack:
A Trilogy of Witch stories and drawings

Brian the Beetroot's Haircut

About Geoff Swift

Geoff is the author of 'The Zak and Rory' series of books, 'The Witch, The Cat and Jack' Trilogy, and 'Brian The Beetroot's Haircut.' He continues researching for The Zak and Rory series, and is enjoying the shared journey with the characters. He has also enjoyed working with Jane Cornwell the Scottish artist and illustrator, who has supported Geoff with the artwork and illustrations in all his books.

Geoff enjoys the outdoors and travelling, is a keen walker, skier and golfer when not writing. Geoff has given primary school talks, loves the engagement, feedback and questions the young learners give.

Listening and engaging with the young learners, Geoff is impressed with their approach to learning and the environment.

As the future of the world is in their hands, the future looks good.

You can follow Geoff's adventures on Twitter: @swift_geoff

And find links to Geoff's other books here: www.geoffswiftwriter.com

Printed in Great Britain
by Amazon